MW01171843

# Thoughts V:

## Leaning into

## the Presence of what is Present

©Herb Stevenson

# Table of Contents

# Thoughts V:

## Leaning Into the Presence of What is Present

# Herb Stevenson

## Healing Den Publishing Company

# Foreword

I am grateful for the attentive support of Hannah Lowe in making the **Thoughts** books possible. Her encouragement has been invaluable.

I am grateful for Mathew and Carolyn Powers for all of their support in writing the first **Thoughts** book as well as in the creation of the healing den program that teaches healing presence.

I am grateful for my wife, Jackie, for her support and sharing of living on our majestic farm with five draft horses, two ponies, two wolf hybrids, and two dogs that create our 500 pounds of security systems. Our combination creates magic every day,

# A Thought

It is not by accident that you are reading this book. Fate is what happens when we are true to who and what we are. Hence, something inside you has accepted the invitation to look at life in a little different way. In doing so, you are opening yourself to a whole new world and a whole new you. Enjoy the trip and share it with someone you love.

Thoughts V is part of a sequel of unknown volumes.

# ONE: HONEY I AM BACK

Tom was looking over some notes from prior meetings with DocKnow as he sat outside in the sun. The temperatures were in the 20s which did not seem to matter as he had a large mug of coffee and his warm Pendleton coat. He was reading....

> "The goal of supporting ourselves, and anyone else is to be in the state of in the moment awareness while the mind becomes silent. Instead of chasing thoughts and/or being consumed by fears, the mind becomes focused solely on the present moment... alert, slightly anxious, and slightly excited. There is silence and stillness, and a continuous, effortless unfolding of energies that might lead to a memory, insight, or revelation. In many respects this is healing."

Suddenly, a roar of an engine coming up the driveway forewarned that DocKnow was back. Walks with Woman had returned a few months ago with White Horse. It had been a quiet time on the ranch...until now.

"Hola" yelled DocKnow as he slid to a stop and then slipped on the ice landing on his bottom with a thud. White Horse and Walks with Woman tried to ask if the was 'okay' between their smirks and belly wiggles. Just as quick DocKnow yelled "where's the coffee" as he jumped up and limped towards the kitchen. Tom got up and walked towards DocKnow as DocKnow veered over to him grabbing the mug of coffee from Tom's hand and saying "thanks" as he gulped it down and added, "a little cold for my taste."

Tom laughed.

All four met in the kitchen to make a fresh pot of coffee and to enjoy DocKnow's return. As often happened with DocKnow, clock-time did not apply. Whether minutes or months, he had the ability to stretch or shrink time to the needs of the moment. This time he shrank time to feel like he had just returned from an hour of running errands even though he had been gone several months.

DocKnow flopped into his chair with a big smile and seemed to warm the faces of all three as we smiled back. We all wondered if he was going to share his latest adventures. Instead, he said, "what you got to eat? Must be dinner time somewhere" as all looked at the clock that said 10:30 am. Prior experiences had indicated it was let's clear the fridge and eat time. As it was, Walks with Woman, White Horse, and Tom drank coffee as DocKnow feasted on more than a fair share of food. When he had finished, he looked at Tom and said, "the phrase you're trying to grasp is 'healing presence'. It's the same calling for every person as they wobble towards their self-awareness."

Tom stuttered for a second then realized he was not the only one caught off guard. Walks with Woman and White Horse seemed a little taken back as they tried to recalibrate their sense of presence to this moment with DocKnow.

DocKnow smiled, "guess I ate too fast. Y'all seem to have been left behind somewhere between the turkey and cold lasagna." All laughed a bit as they recalibrated their sense of the presence of what is present to connect with each other. As they did so, the conversation shifted to chit chat and what has been happening at the farm since he left. It seemed like DocKnow was getting us ready for what was coming.

The rest of the day was filled with teasing and a deep sense of gratitude for each other. As they all called it a day, it dawned on Tom that the depth of connection to another person leaves an energetic void that we call missing the other person when they are not physically present. He realized that this is also true when people as energetically absent even though physically present. He pondered if this is normal existence where most people focus on the absence to what is present.

# TWO: MEANING MAKING

The next day, Tom and DocKnow went for a walk around the pasture and down into the glacial rocks and cliffs on the farm. These ancient wisdom carriers were pushed from northern Canada during the ice age. These rock travelers were comprised of billions of quartz stones emitting regenerative energy for all plants and animals. People simply felt better when they came onto the property without knowing that their energetic frequency was being elevated and dissolving any pent-up anger, resentment, or other lower vibrational energies.

DocKnow paused in front of the cliffs and said, "these were likely ceremonial grounds." Tom nodded assuming he was likely correct and waited for the next loaded phrase. Instead DocKnow continued to walk along the path against the sheer rock walls towering above them.

Suddenly, Tom felt like he had gone through a veil that revealed the sense of the ancient presence embedded in these massive rocks and cliffs. He was understanding that rocks were often referred to as the wisdom carriers because not only have they endured millions of years on earth, they captured the energies of those times…all of them.

"Tends to disorient one when walking though the veils of the presence of what is present," said DocKnow. Tom was startled then smiled as he realized that the teaching while walking was to always to aware of the presence of what is present, even if it is by hiding in one's mind trying to make meaning according to socially constructed rule.

# THREE: HOW WE
# TELL OUR STORIES

As they headed back to the farmhouse, DocKnow began a teaching,

"Living in the present moment is a paradoxical experience. Generally, people see, think, feel, and react to every moment in every day. There is not an existential experience beyond what is being interpreted in the mind. In other words, we tell ourselves a multitude of stories every day without being aware of everything else that is present. Hence, we are locked in the prison of our minds by learning to only focus on socially defined 'important things.' Once, we learn to color our perceptions outside the lines of socially constructed rules, we invite a deeper experience of the presence of what is present."

After an extended pause to breathe deeply, he continued. "Generally, learning to reveal our socially constructed world is to be able to witness how we make meaning, which also means how we ignore the multitude of other possibilities that exist in any moment. So, the first step is to understand how we make meaning. A useful tool to support one to examine their thinking processes is the "ladder of inference" method, originally developed by Chris Argyris. The ladder of inference is probably the most commonly used, and most effective, technique to evaluate and improve cognitive and communicative styles. In basic terms the ladder of inference involves the following seven steps which are a socially constructed way to make meaning..

1. I observe "data."
2. I then select data from what I have observed.
3. I add meaning to the data from a personal and cultural perspective.
4. I make assumptions based on the meaning that I have added.
5. I draw conclusions based on our assumptions.
6. I adopt beliefs based on my conclusions.
7. Finally, I take action based on my conclusions."

## Telling Our Story

DocKnow said "when we move beyond the cognitive to examine a little deeper, and add the emotional fuel that drives embedded in the process, as suggested by Kerry Patterson, Joseph Grenny, Ron McMillan, and Al Switzler in their bestselling books Crucial Conversations and Crucial Confrontations, the model becomes a clear explanation of our cognitive, emotive, and communication processes, especially during our more explosive and possibly embarrassing moments."

This model suggests that in every situation we have four overriding processes that help us decide what has happened and what action to take. As shown below, this model adds a feeling step to the process.

See and Hear → → → Tell a Story → → → Feel → → → Act

DocKnow continued, "the concept of the ladder of inference integrated with "how we tell our stories" can help us and our clients identify the steps in their reasoning that may lead to unintended consequences. The ladder of inference focuses on how people come to take the actions they take. When the structure of our thinking and feeling processes from Patterson et. al. are overlain with the ladder of inference as a meta-model, clarity becomes expanded and adds the feeling or emotional dimension to the model. The combined model would look like the following:

**I See and Hear**

1. I observe "data."
2. I then select data from what I have observed.

**I Tell a Story**

3. I add meaning to the data from a personal and cultural perspective.
4. I make assumptions based on the meaning that I have added.
5. I draw conclusions based on my assumptions.
6. I adopt beliefs based on my conclusions.

**I apply a Feeling Response–Automatically or Consciously**

7. I create emotional reactions that are congruent with the Story I have told myself.

**I Take Action**

8. Finally, I take actions based on my conclusions and emotional reactions.

Tom noted that "the models individually and combined as one create a process to witness and interrupt the learned sequence leading to meaning making and to the actions taken. Witnessing shifts the process from unconscious habits to conscious awareness and choices."

"Exactly" said DocKnow "and it enables one to slow down the witnessing even further to reveal the presence of what is present for that individual. In other words, the ability to see how one originally constructed the meaning-making and emotional reactions loaded onto the meaning. We can begin to deconstruct our habitual patterns locked in the prison of the mind and begin to become present moment to moment."

Tom was digesting as fast as he could until he said, "so when we find the meaning-making constructs and attend to that process and any emotional reactions, we can begin to disassemble how we have made meaning in our own particular way? Moreover, we can examine if we truly believe how we have assumed the world actually functions."

DocKnow added, "a short cut to our unconscious processes is to attend to the energies that arise whether it is dissociation or rage or something else." Tom pondered for a while, then asked, "if we are able to be attentive to the moment on an ongoing basis, witnessing the reactive energies that drive our meaning making, we can begin to isolate and change the habitualized scripts we have created as our socially constructed reality."

DocKnow nodded.

# FOUR: PAYING ATTENTION

DocKnow sat down at the table where they were drinking coffee. He asked Tom if he had any questions about the discussion of how we make meaning. Tom thought about and wondered "is there a simple way to describe how meaning making and emotions are merged over time?"

DocKnow said "if we examine meaning-making as a stage of development, based on what a person is paying attention to, it is possible to shed some light on how we create our meaning-making processes.. Note I said shed some light." chuckled DocKnow.

"Let's start with a refresh of presence of what is present as a beginning point. Our presence matters for how we experience people and places are made manifest— how they come into our awareness. This applies to people, places, animals, or things. In essence, when we engage with the world, in the early stages our awareness is quite narrow to what is present beyond our experiences and self-created meaning making. As our attention expands, we can become aware of more than the thoughts and emotions we have constructed in our minds. Thus the stages of paying attention is like a developmental line that spirals into greater awareness of the presence of what is present within ourself, others, the environment."

Tom thought about his own developing journey and realized he had learned over a series of developmental processes, that it is hard to be generous, disciplined, or patient when he was not fully present to more than his learned existence. He realized further that when he was present to himself and the world, he became more flexible, and more receptive to the environment around himself. Finally, he blurted out "the more present we are, the more we can tune in to what is happening." DocKnow smiled, and then proceeded.

"There is a basic series of steps of what a person pays attention to or makes meaning as they develop over time." DocKnow said, "initially we learn to pay attention to what makes one feel safe and often see themselves as 'me in you,' a form of mirroring others, so as to safely orient in relation to the world. This can translate into such things as talking nicely, being confluent with others and being worried about their self-image. In a way, it is as if the person is looking for themselves in others. Tom recalled his younger years when he had behaved this way. It was like trying to discover his own path and somewhere along the way had lost his own map. He had slowly conformed to what was expected of him and lost his own sense of self.
DocKnow continued. "This leads to the next stage of paying attention that could be construed as a beginning of differentiation and therefore one sees the world as 'me or you'. Many struggle in this stage as differentiation creates tension and the rise of debate or defending oneself. Often this process can be experienced as self-righteousness for others because the struggle with separating identity from their point of view is enmeshed."

Tom paused DocKnow to run to the used coffee room and grab a fresh cup of coffee. As he plopped into his chair, spilling half the coffee onto the table creating a scurry of chairs moving quickly away from the table, Tom said, "whoops." After many sopping paper towels, Tom continued, "I can see these stages and they are kind of fuzzy in the sense that I recognize when I was predominantly in one or the other as well as on occasion, I slip back into them."

DocKnow smiled and said, "the wisdom of these examples of stages is it is about what are you unconsciously focusing your attention on" DocKnow paused and suggested they continue to create more clarity.

"Hopefully, development continues as one is exposed to things like the ladder of inference where they become more reflective and can conceive their world as 'you and me'. Notice the shift is away from oneself to both/and thinking."

Tom remembered that when he originally met DocKnow he was quite combative and very either/or thinking. Since then, DocKnow had opened Tom's eyes to a wider, broader, deeper level of perceptions that was reflective, more discerning and less judgmental.

DocKnow continued, "finally, as attentiveness continues to expand, there becomes an awareness that the world is emergent and generative. One becomes aware of and attentive to the presence of what is present."

Tom reflected on this stage and realized that when began to engage or be embraced by the ceremonial energies of the medicine wheel, he had experienced a sense of "we" as in wholeness and oneness at the same, where we were both separate and together.

"These stages might look something like this" as DocKnow slid a diagram across the table. They are slightly different for every person; however, it reminds us to pay attention to what we are paying attention to. Moreover, he realized that in the fourth stage, the presence of what is present revealed itself deeply inside him as he felt united with everything.

Tom said, "so, when I feel that someone is really listening to me, I feel more alive, I feel our true selves coming to the surface.

"Exactly" said DocKnow.

| Field of Attention | Field Dynamic | Internal World |
|---|---|---|
| "Me in You" | **Creating Safety** | Not saying what I think. |
| | Talking Nice | *I am Speaking from What I think you want to hear.* |
| | Confluent/Mirroring | Polite routines; Empty phrases |
| | I in Me | View is on myself |
| | Worried about self-image | I am looking for me in you |
| "Me or you" | **Debate or Defend** | Saying what I think of you |
| | Talking Tough | *I am speaking from what I think* (you need or how I can be |
| | Differentiated/Separated | helpful or how I can look good)) |
| | "I in It" You are an Object | Divergent Views (tinge of self-righteousness) |
| | Trying to Establish self-image | I am my point of view (of what is needed) separate from you |
| | Of oneself | Either/Or thinking |
| "Me and you" | **Dialogue** | Pause, observe, reflect, choose. |
| | **Reflective Inquiry** | *Speaking from seeing myself as part of the whole* (process). |
| | Talking with | Empathic. |
| | Inclusive/encompassing | Discernment replaces judgements. |
| | "I in Thou" Your are a person | I am me as you are you |
| | Accepting myself separate from | We have different viewpoints |
| | a public image | Either/or thinking replaced with Both/and |
| "We" | **Presence** | Emergent and Generative: 1 + 1 = 3 |
| | **Emergent & Generative** | *Speaking from You and me become we* leading to stillness, |
| | Talking As | collective creativity, flow and collective presence. |
| | Integrative/Holistic | Energy releases, Identity shifts, Sense of authenticity |
| | "I in Now" We | Deep awareness that **We** are one and Separate at some |
| | Being myself from a place of | deep energetic level. |
| | Presence | Sense of Spiritual kinship |

"As we develop our sense of presence, we begin to realize that presence or being present is a developmental process. Our awareness expands beyond our internal world. We broaden our perspective. We engage the broader world through a series of stages as indicated in the images and descriptions above," said DocKnow. "Here's a reflective tool to support your understanding how you have developed your stages of paying attention," as he slid a second piece of paper across the table.

Please describe how you see your personal development coincides with each stage.

| Stages | My understanding of the stage through examples | My understanding of what I can and will do different as I develop more presence |
|---|---|---|
| Me in You | | |
| Me or You | | |
| You & Me | | |
| We | | |

Tom studied the diagram and identified himself in different stages of his life. He knew that DocKnow would consider it wise for him to spend time with the reflective questions so that he could identify and begin to create an awareness of the shifts he has completed and could be next in his internalized perceptions. He realized that the presence of what is present involves every aspect of life including listening.

# FIVE: DEEPENING
# THE REFRAME

Tom reflected on the stages of "what and how one pays attention." As they sat and chit chatted for the next hour, he pondered and realized that paying attention to what he was paying attention to was more than a simple exercise. It required daily discipline to focus the mind and to be able to witness what his mind was doing. At some level, he had known it but now realized it in his bones.

White Horse was sitting at the table with Tom, as he looked up and saw White Horse quizzically looking at him. "Something got ahold of you," he asked. Tom nodded and shared his insight about paying attention to what and how one was paying attention seemed like a lot of discipline and hard work. "It is" said White Horse, "like unlearning all the programmed bad habits used to make-meaning and to perceive what one believes to be true in order to see what is truly in front of you. For example, listening is one of the least well practiced behaviors that creates confusion as most people are speaking from learned scripts from the past. Generally, the average person stops listening to the other person at about 20% into the conversation and begin to scan their mind for the "learned" response. If they are in stage one of paying attention, they will respond confluently, etc. for each stage of paying attention. Correspondingly, there are four stages of listening that overlap or permeate the stages of paying attention."

Tom's head wobbled for a second as he realized that this paying attention to what he was paying attention to applied to his entire paradigm of being himself. His face contorted as he pondered these insights resulting in White Horse laughing himself silly. "Guess we struck a nerve or something," said White Horse when he composed himself. Tom did not laugh as he was struggling to reorient himself to this much broader perspective of presence and reality. Then, he remembered looking into the deep sky and waiting until he felt like he was one with it. He reckoned that this is the 4$^{th}$ stage of paying attention.

As they settled into dinner, it became quiet at the table while Tom's mind was noisier than a freight train with squeaky wheel. Thoughts were bouncing around like an out-of-control pinball machine. He was tired and yet wide awake. Maybe it was weariness from an overload of energy, information, or presence.

He realized he was completely discombobulated. He went to bed.

# SIX: LISTENING TO WHAT

The next morning, Tom awoke to the instantaneous chorus of hundreds of birds singing. He smiled as he felt this moment is a blessing to anyone who is able to wake up before dawn with the windows open. As he focused his attention, the singing became louder as he wondered if the ancient saying that this singing is what creates the sunrise. As told to him, the "birds were literally singing up the sun." As he listened further, he noticed that his mind was completely quiet as if uninterested in the sunrise or the singing. "Huh" he mumbled aloud, as he got out of bed and headed for the shower.

After his shower, he got dressed and went into the kitchen. Breakfast was on the table, or at least, what was left. He realized that everyone was on the porch eating, so he filled his plate with eggs, bacon, biscuits, and gravy, then joined them. As he sat down, he noted heads down and everyone chewing with an ecstatic look on their faces. He joined them in the silence. In a moment, he understood the looks on their faces. The flavors were better described in noises and smiles, and heavenly nods.

# SEVEN: HEARING

After clearing the table and doing the dishes, White Horse and Walks with Woman went to the barn to tend to the horses. They needed feed, water, and the manure cleaned. Tom looked at DocKnow and then jumped off the porch to help with the chores. His mind was tired, and he wanted to move a bit including shoveling manure. As he grabbed a manure rake from the Kubota utility vehicle, he looked into the sky and felt a tingling energy of oneness fill his heart, he had an overwhelming feeling of gratitude. No reason, just gratitude of being.

For the next hour, White Horse complained that manure for draft horses was directly in proportion to the 2600 pounds of animal. In other words, gigundus. Tom laughed as he focused on the lightheartedness between White Horse and Walks with Woman. It seemed that they like to tease each other.

When returned to the house, DocKnow was gone, and he left a nice for Walks with Woman and White Horse to chat about listening as a form of paying attention to what is present. They got coffee and sat on the porch as the four dogs joined them lying on the floor between and on them. Maya the mastiff preferred to lean against people rather than lying by herself. Many time they had wondered if this was her way of giving and getting hugs. Smart dog if true.

Walks with Woman started the conversation. "As DocKnow has described the four stages of paying attention, there are corresponding developmental stages of listening. This is not to be confused with hearing…hearing is making meaning of noise and listening involves presence." This made sense to Tom as he often thought some people made a lot of noise, he chuckled.

"Ahem", barked Walks with Woman as she recalled Tom's attention to this moment. He nodded to her that he was paying attention as she continued.

"The first level of listening is a range of hearing to listening with an agenda. Sound is occurring, but it is not receiving any of your attention. This means that you can't really listen effectively with the TV on in the background, reading the newspaper or while you are texting on your phone. A slight variation of this process of hearing has been construed occasionally as hearing with an agenda. Listening from the assumption that you already know what is being said, therefore you listen only to confirm your own meaning and judgments. A further distinction can be found in indigenous cultures where not listening is an existential act of indicating that the person does not exist or does not deserve to be heard. If intentional it becomes a form of shunning when the focus is ceremonial or ritual such as in modern day would be a "big" decision is being made or the community is in dialogue where all voices are to be honored and heard and some are ignored."

Tom focused on the nuances of what Walks with Woman said. As he scanned his own life, he could relate where he had been guilty of not listening or hearing with an agenda. He winced when he realized that not listening is an existential and energetic act of disrespect that has been enculturated as acceptable behavior as evidenced by its prevalence. Tom looked at Walks with Woman and White Horse and said, "in other words, the absence of my paying attention to what I am paying attention to creates a feeling of disconnection for the other person." Tom now understood that his lack of attention or absence of presence is disrespectful. He recalled his own experiences of being treated as if his voice did not matter. It felt like being treated as if he did not exist or was not important enough to be listened to. His body remembered this feeling deeply and very disconcertedly.

# EIGHT: REACTIVE

After a bio-break and some lighthearted chit chat while playing with the dogs, the three sat down. The two wolf hybrids, shepherd looking wolves, came over for their morning attention. Lots of petting, scratching, and shedding later, White Horse continued the conversation. "Because listening directly impacts what one is paying attention to, the second level of listening is about hearing what's in your mind, often in rebuttal to whatever is being said by another person.  You are engaged in conversation, but your attention is not on the words that are being said by your partner. Your attention is on the voice in your head that is reacting to what your partner said and planning the next thing you want to say. In other words, you don't really hear and acknowledge what your partner said, but instead jump to what the little voice in your head has to say about what your partner said. Yes, the little voice in your head that just went "What little voice in my head?" exaggerated White Horse as he looked squarely into Tom's eyes. Tom did not appreciate the humor as the truth about the little voice stung a bit.

Wanting to make sure Tom was clear, Walks with Woman added, "this listening is when you pay attention to what is different, novel, or disquieting from what you already know in preparation to allow the little voice in your mind to rebut, refute, and sway the conversation into another direction."

Tom noted he understood and thought "I really did not need that extra emphasis."

As Tom pondered, he wondered what was next.

White Horse continued, "for some indigenous tribes, facts and details are collected while energetically seeking a potential connection to past, present, and future. Facts are understood within the tribal collective rather than the individual's perceptions. Listening to respectfully experience by hearing through one's entire set of senses to understand the person or situation before one decides to answer."

Tom realized that even at the early stages of listening, the focus of paying attention to one's attention had impact on conversations and moreover shifted the focus from within one's own stories and to include the stories of the community and therefore beyond himself.

# NINE : EMPATHIC (CELLULAR) HEARING

They broke for lunch. Turkey sandwiches, jalapeno chips and lots of coffee vanished quickly. Each walked a bit around the farm to release the pent-up energy from sitting so long. Tom decided to play tag with the dogs and was being chased and knocked down to loud laughing and barking. As they sat down, Walks with Woman suggested iced tea for a change, and all poured a hefty glass for themselves.

Walks with Woman looked at White Horse and Tom as each nodded, they were ready. "Listening at this level is referred to as cellular or empathic hearing. You register more than just the words the person is saying. You can feel/sense the emotion they are communicating. You can detect if they are angry, or sad, or excited. In other words, you are sharing a piece of the other person's experience. You demonstrate that you are listening with your body: you may be making eye contact, nodding your head, leaning forward, are all signs that you are connected and present. You are beginning to listen as your more present to the person and yourself in this moment.

Tom thought about times he had felt this way. He realized that his frequent experiences were with White Horse, Walks with Woman, and DocKnow. He scanned his memory which triggered a feeling of being connected to them energetically during those moments.

White Horse added to the conversation, "it is seeing something through another person's eyes. Cellular hearing is empathic listening and is when one pays attention to the energies and feelings of the other person in an accepting way.  It opens the listener and allows an experience of "standing in the other's shoes" to take place. Attention shifts to, allowing for deep connection."

Tom allowed this sense of being present to recognize that the more present one becomes the better one listens. Presence directly correlates with listening.

Walks with Woman added, "with a quiet mind, a sense of the other person becomes clearer energetically as well as through hearing the words. Empathy becomes meaning-making information as it is experienced through related prior experiences that expands to the heart to form compassion for the other while maintaining clear boundaries of oneself and other. It is like honoring another's journey without becoming it."

Tom surrendered to the feeling of being connected to the energies of the words especially "honoring another's journey without becoming it." He wondered how many times he had dishonored other's journey by trying to become it or influence it. He felt humbled.

# TEN: NURTURING

Walks with Woman went to feed the horses while White Horse drove to the grocery to get some food for dinner. Tom decided to sit in the setting sun enjoying the quiet filled with the wind blowing through the trees. He wondered about how little people really listen, and more impactful for him, how most people are not present. Instead, they exist in the prison of their minds living by the rules learned over time and not ever engaging with life beyond their prisms of perceptions. "Hey snoozer" yelled White Horse. As Tom was startled. Apparently, he had fallen asleep. "Dinner" called Walks with Woman as she set the table. White Horse brought glasses of water for everyone as they sat down. Tom looked over the table and realized they were eating at Colonel Sanders tonight. Fried chicken mashed potatoes, corn, green beans, and gravy. As Tom looked further, he saw the freshly made biscuits at the end of the table. The room became very quiet as each seemed to be listening to their taste buds and stomachs as the feast was consumed.

# ELEVEN: CONNECTIVE LISTENING

After breakfast and the chores, DocKnow came driving up in a cloud of dust. He jumped out of the truck and headed directly to the used coffee room and then to the coffee pot. After a healthy gulp, he murmured, "better make another pot, I drove all night". As they sat in suspended time while DocKnow kept singing, "I left my butt in San Francisco" everyone else was wondering if he was entertaining himself or trying to get a reaction from us. It quickly ended when he plopped down and said, "let's get started."

DocKnow listened while White Horse and Walks with Woman explained what had been discussed. After refilling his coffee, DocKnow started, "at this ultimate level of listening, you are actually able to hear the commitment or desire behind what others are saying. This doesn't come from thinking about why they said what they said. It is something that you just know because you are so present in that moment your intuition just picks up on it. You feel it. When we are totally present and listening, it is possible to know things through the shared experience." DocKnow paused to see how the information was being absorbed. Then he continued, "this deeper level of listening is difficult to express in linear language. It is a state of being in which everything slows down and inner wisdom is accessed. In interpersonal communication, it is described as oneness and flow."

Tom thought about this level of listening as he sought experiences that would correlate, then he remembered how he felt during different sweatlodges. He often felt as if he experienced the prayers of others as a sense of deep knowing without paying attention to the words. It was like he was attuned to energetic vibrations of the person.

DocKnow added that "from an indigenous perspective, this level of listening is generative and co-creative. A dance between the energetic connections of the body, mind, and soul evolves where presence balances vulnerability. Courage and compassion unite into two individuals and a dyad each experiencing and being experienced. The connection is a form of spiritual understanding and knowing that increases respect for individual humanity and oneness between. Listening is generative and Co-Creating where the higher connection begins to impact each other's life journey as a binding relationship in physical, mental, emotional, and/or spiritual dimensions."

Tom grappled within himself until his mind suddenly became quiet. He began to experience a deep sense of knowing the energy behind the concepts as if the words were not relevant by the presence embedded in the words was alive. It felt like two people listening at this level were within the presence of what is present to each other as well as the surrounding environment. Wholeness and oneness all at once.

As he was sitting aglow with the feeling of this level of listening, he recognized that it was entwined with the stages of paying attention to. As paying attention developed, he realized that it was coincidental with a sense of becoming more of who one is. This led him to wonder is there a process between each level that supports maturing into the next higher stage of paying attention and therefore to generative listening.

# TWELVE: BETWEEN STAGES

The next morning seemed to be unusual. It was deadly quiet. Tom wondered what was going on. He got up and walked around. Outside was Mel Torme, the infamous jazz singer, singing a jazz riff of Do Be Do Be Do. Tom was confused by the whole situation. What was Mel Torme doing being here? Why was he singing one of his famous jazz riffs? Amongst the confusion, he heard Walks with Woman say "time to wake up. Your singing sucks."

Tom opened one eye and realized he had been dreaming. Strange dream he thought. Stranger that he was singing such a nonsensical song. He rolled out of bed with a thud as he lost his footing and hit the floor. "Not fun" he mumbled as the others heard his thud and all started laughing. "Do be do be do be" echoed in his mind as he got up, showered and headed for breakfast.

DocKnow, White Horse, and Walks with Woman were smirking and said, "clearly you are not a jazz singer." Tom acknowledged the humor as he drank his coffee even though he was still confused about what the dream represented.

# THIRTEEN: DO-BE

After breakfast, DocKnow asked, "have you figured out your dream?"

"Nah" replied Tom as he was not ready for more humor at his expense as he looked across the table to see DocKnow.

DocKnow said "your dream describes the process that occurs between the stages of developing for paying attention as well as for listening. The jazz riff of Mel Torme is the sequence of developing more presence. We literally do be do be do be between stages as we move forward with more presence. Stages move through phases of awareness development as one is learning to consciously witness oneself. Being aware and then learning to stay grounded in who you are and not what you've been told you are is a process of do then be. In other words, it is an interactive process of learning to do something, then developing more self-awareness leading to a deeper sense of presence and being. Once this occurs, the Do Be phase of a stage of development moves to the next level. For example, let's apply this to when you developed your healing presence using stones and crystals."

DocKnow Paused to see if Tom was grasping the process. Tom nodded okay, so the proceeded.

The first stage of developing healing techniques is called UNTO. Using the Do-Be model, phase one is do unto and phase two is be unto. In the Do UNTO phase one learns a basic technique approach to healing. It can be mechanical and is guided by inner voices (external authority) seeking to remember how to do it. Often the internal world is performance (do correct) focused. Occasionally, at this phase their might be a driving motivation where one sees their self as savior, hero, gifted healer; however, they can fall into the trap of 'must be the expert' so as to allay any concerns for fear of embarrassment. Due to the basic insecurity of just learning, might not accept challenges from clients well. Very little presence."

Tom thought about this phase and winced. He remembered bouncing between what he had experienced, what he had learned, and what he feared. He felt very insecure and was very dogmatic in how he followed the exact instructions of how to work with rocks and crystals. As he recalled, he had repeated the same process when learning energy healing and then remembered this was pretty much every time, he was learning something new. He liked that he could see his own process from a different perspective than amid the actual learning.

DocKnow continued, "the second phase of the UNTO Stage is Be Unto. As we developed a sense of confidence in what to do, some latitude develops in how to do which shifts to a be unto mode. This is often represented by consuming or overwhelming clients with open heartedness or spiritual energy. In such cases, one is not present to the healing energies and can get lost in ungrounded energies with no or low boundaries separating from client. This can trigger client to feel exposed or ungrounded or to simply dissociate while the healer is in a state of euphoria or confusion."

Tom recalled a very difficult experience when he traveled with Walks with Woman to Israel. He had taken his rocks and crystals at her encouragement. The first disconcerting challenge was the Israelis were unsure what to do with a long-haired dude with a bag of rocks. After much bantering, they decided to allow him to board the plane and fly to Tel Aviv. When at Tel Aviv, Walks with Woman was at teaching a workshop. Between classes, she encouraged the students to experience the healing stones. One person, Yael, seemed to travel to another dimension and was having a complete out of body experience. Unaware of such experiences, Tom was shocked into action. He removed the stones, and in one particular case, pried from her hands a large quartz crystal. Slowly, he brought her back to her body. Having no idea what else to do, he sat her down beside a tree in hopes that she would become grounded. He shuttered from remembering that experience.

As he came out of the memory, he saw DocKnow smiling. "Shall we continue" said DocKnow. Tom nodded. DocKnow continued. "The second stage is ON BEHALF which include the phase do for on behalf and Be for on behalf."

"Do for phase involves traditional healing models and practices, where the person is the healer, the expert. The person has developed a strong sense of confidence based on years of practice and as a result they have technical expertise to create healing results for many: however, it is still predominantly technique based and they tend to work mostly from muscle memory and less from presence."

Tom recalled a period where he felt overly confident because he knew he knew the techniques and the client feedback was very positive. It never occurred to him that the power was embedded in the ancient healing practice and not him.

DocKnow sensed the situation and continued, "the next phase is Be For on behalf. It is the beginning to self-embody healing presence in understanding of the creation of sacred space. Typically, the healer does not quite understand healing presence as a state of being; however, they do know how to create strong sacred space but might get ungrounded or unable to hold the ceremonial sacred space. This is because with being fully grounded in themselves, they can get lost in the feeling of sacred space and try to hold onto it".

Tom said, "this was the stage or phase where I became humble." He continued, "I was energized and quite full of myself walking around like a little wizard. I handed stones and crystal out like candy and watched their energies shift. Some happy with the playfulness and others not liking being toyed with."

Tom continued, "I attended a workshop with the world renowned psychic and energy healer, Rosalyn Bruyere, who kindly called me aside and said 'you are doing unto people without their permission. Healing is self-empowering'. Tom realized that at that moment he had completely changed his process and mindset. Healing comes inside the person not from me."

As a constant reminder of her wise blessing, Tom noted "Rosalyn had referred to him as the Mad Wizard from Cleveland and he has continued to remember that he should be focused on supporting the healing from within the clients and not any magic he might be able to conjure."

DocKnow gave a deep knowing look to Tom as if they were enjoined at some energetic level of awareness. Tom was not sure if they had had past lives together or similar stages of development, but he had never felt closer to DocKnow than now.

DocKnow suggested they break for a later lunch as it was already midday. Tom realized that it felt like a long minute instead of several hours. He recalled DocKnow talking in the past about stretching and shrinking time by moving into liminal space, where there is no time. He let go of that thought as soup and sandwiches were brought to the table. Tom jumped up and went to the bathroom to freshen up and clear his head. He returned to laughs and guffaws as he watched a pitcher of lemonade pour over the table and onto DocKnow. Tom decided not to ask what happened as DocKnow did not seem pleased. He quietly sat down and started eating.

# FOURTEEN: WITH

After a shower and change of clothes, DocKnow returned to the table freshly cleaned and no residual fly attracting sticky lemonade to be seen. White Horse and Walks with Woman continued to smirk throughout dinner and Tom decided to not inquire about what had happened.

After the late lunch was cleared, it was horse feeling time, so all took a break. Tom sat under a tree with the two wolf hybrids lying beside him. He was pondering his journey and how the do-be stages so clearly explained his own developmental journey.

DocKnow suggested continuing for a short time, and Tom recalled short could feel like a minute and be hours. "Stage three is With. It involves the phase of Do With (collaborate, maybe enjoin) and Be With (Presence). It is at this stage, like the stages of paying attention or listening, presence begins to permeate the healing process and one's existence.

Do With initiates the healing presence where developing through enjoining energies with the client, via collaborative participation. Clients might not be comfortable because they are asked to maintain eye contact and fully participate in the healing process such as actively engaged, consciously through witnessing and tracking sensations. The healer supports the client as surprised emotions might surface for client and healer. It is at this phase that the healing practitioners can reach a level as awareness of the healing container is not them, it is the energy of presence."

Tom was fumbling around as if the insight was directly in front of him and his eyes were unable to clearly focus. Tom reflected then asked, "is this when the healer or ceremonial leader begins to engage the healing process as presence, like the beginning of creating and being a healing presence? It feels like just before energetically becoming part of the sweatlodge energy through prayers and invocations."

DocKnow nodded and then added, "many do not reach this stage or once they do, they lose their ability to surrender to the energies and try to chase the process mechanically by regressing to prior stages."

Tom could understand how instead of surrendering to grow into the next phase, the mind could see it as a shiny object that it tries to own. He had experienced this many times like a two steps forward, three steps backwards, and four steps sideways as he had tried to own the energies and associated feelings instead of being with them.

DocKnow realized that Tom was in the energies of what was being discussed as he was using his memory as a map to travel to prior experiences and relive them in this moment, where he was much more present.

DocKnow continued, "Be With is the next phase. The courage to be fully present without preconceived notions, creates the window of perception to open to the moment as consciously aware presence. It can present by surrendering or more accurately to allow in the presence of what is present. This is enacted as bare or naked attention to witness oneself and the other person. Liminal space can open for oneself and the client as a healing presence. Because sacred space permeates oneself and the other person, presence opens the point of power in the moment for self-healing, dissolving old wounds, stories, and attachments. These energies move towards a state of BEING for the client, healer, and essence of each."

Tom realized that this state requires a form of being with that literally means being within the presence of what is present for oneself, others, and all that is in that moment. It is being in the stillness of the silence that awakens the power of the present moment and anyone in it to heal. Though he had experienced it on occasion, he wondered if it was possible to be with all the time.

DocKnow interrupted Tom. "It is possible to be with in any

moment with focused attention and the discipline to allow in the presence of what is present, the state of being in the moment. And it requires dedication to end a lot of stories and imprints that hide in the recesses of the mind." Tom was not sure if he entirely understood and yet he sensed the truth in it.

DocKnow allowed Tom to meander through his experiences resonating in this moment, then added. "There is one additional state not often referred to as it is more difficult. It is Be (Healing Presence), then he paused and said let's take a break."

Tom was curious and noticed his tiredness, which he was not sure was due to the conversation or the increasing levels of vibration that seemed to fill him with each successive stage and phase. He wondered if DocKnow was invoking these higher frequencies to expand his capacity to know and be in them. Over the years, he had suspected that DocKnow was able to do that, raise the energetic frequency of the field as a sacred (liminal) space for learning. Tom got up from the table and realized they had been sitting for hours. He stretched and groaned as DocKnow yelled at him "getting old?!?" as he walked into the house.

They relaxed for the rest of the day, which meant they attended to fixing some broken fence rails, repairing the barn siding and enjoying the outdoor air. For Tom, it felt like he was simmering inside while working outside. DocKnow often referred to this as sitting in the cauldron of one's own making, where one tends to forget that not only are they in the cauldron, but they are also supplying the fuel to do the cooking.

# FIFTEEN: BE

The next morning was filled with the normal chores before breakfast. Waking at 5:30 am, getting the dogs out for the day, lighting the fire to heat the house, and making lots of coffee. Then, it was off to feed the horses and shovel the manure. Walks with Woman and White Horse worked together with Tom and got it all done in less than an hour. White Horse complained the entire time about the amount of manure and Tom simply decided to let him complain as it seemed to satisfy something inside him; maybe, to irritate Walks with Woman.

They return to the house for a lighthearted conversation over breakfast. Once they ate to your content, typically mostly coffee, they all sat down to start the day.

DocKnow suggested that Walks with Woman start the conversation as Tom looked at White Horse. Both shrugged their shoulders and leaned into their chairs.

Walks with Woman started by saying "the key to truly understanding and moving through the stages and phases of Do-Be is to return to center or if lucky to move into the center of your being on occasion while moving through the stages." Walks with Woman paused to see if this was registering with Tom. DocKnow said, "this might help" as he slid a diagram onto the table.

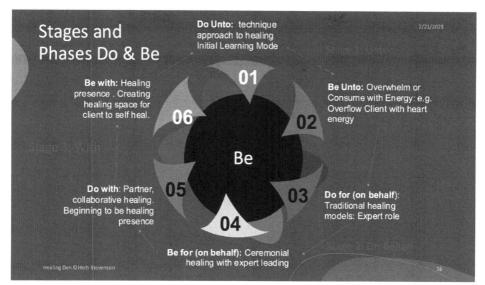

Walks with Woman smiled and nodded to DocKnow as she continued.

"As can be seen from the diagram, most people follow a circular path in their developmental process. This enables one to use time as a measure in their journey; however, within the center of this circular path is BE. It consists of sufficient conscious awareness to surrender in a moment to the living presence of what is present. It is experienced as a state of silence as in no mind with clarity of awareness of knowing and being. There is no need to do only BE. It enables one to access or source all three stages and the six phases interacting simultaneously. These stages and phases are recognized as holistic energies expanding and integrating in the natural movement towards Being."

DocKnow slid a second diagram onto the table and said, "that might look like this."

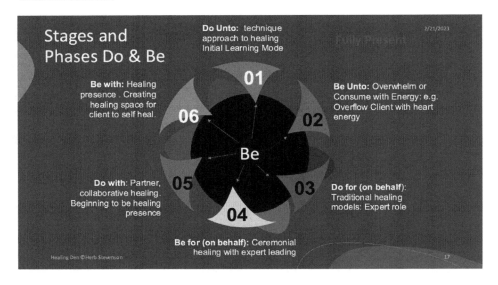

Tom looked at the diagram and immediately realized that time creates the illusion of chronological sequencing when at the center of ourselves, like reflected in the medicine wheel, we are our true self when centered and living in the presence of what is present. He realized that the discipline of being present through meditation and prayer would eventually open this door. It also added another dimension of understanding the simultaneous development of the coinciding evolving and emerging self. Another way of looking at the DO-BE developmental process is that doing with discipline is the evolving self and being with present consistent with one's heart's desire is the emerging self. Everything leads to the unfolding of true self.

DocKnow looked at Tom and asked White Horse if he would like to add something. White Horse studied Tom for a very long moment, then said, "ceremony, rituals, prayers, and meditation are methods to open the door deep within oneself to the state of Being. The mind constructed in sequential time tries to prevent the discipline and practice that leads to experience being, unless trained with the full commitment required to listening to the calling and echoes of one's own heart."

Tom felt that these were words of truth coming from a deep sense of knowing and moreover of remembering something ancient.

He focused on the energies he was experiencing in his body. As it felt like he was being imprinted with a resonance he had not experienced.

# SIXTEEN: IMPRINTS (TIME CRYSTALS)

The four of them had called it a day or night as time felt compressed with insights and energies that required Tom more than a moment to get comfortable. He had pondered the diagrams and realized that time is a construct to uniformly structure the moments of each day to support organized societies. He felt OK with the thought of this artificial organization that supports work, schools, religions, and all organizations to do whatever they do. One thought that stuck in Tom's crawl was what gets in the way of finding the center, of being, as indicated in the Do-Be diagram and the invisible intent of most ceremonies. He knew he needed to unravel or reveal or understand this, what seemed to be, universal condition of mankind.

As the morning unfolded, Tom explained to Walks with Woman, DocKnow, and White Horse his concern or inquiry about what prevents most people from being. All three looked at him, and in unison said, "imprints." Tom choked on their answer and started waving his hand in a motion attempting to encourage them to elaborate as he tried to clear his throat. He became quite comical as he was gagging and flailing his arms while knocking over the chair trying to go inside to get a glass of water. When he came back, Tom was still trying to clear his throat while his eyes were watering amidst trying to look composed, NOT.

DocKnow was still smiling as he teased, "not sure if you are allergic to imprints or you were taken by surprise or both." Walks with Woman, and White Horse were smirking as DocKnow shifted the focus to this moment. "Throughout our lives we are etched with a mixture of energies that can become imprints. These imprints are often referred to as introjects in psychology where energy and behavioral norms are forced onto a person without the opportunity to decide and determine the validity of the energy and behavior. For example, most children are forced to learn basic safety rules such as don't cross the street except in a crosswalk and only after looking both ways for traffic." DocKnow paused to see if Tom was following the concepts. He continued, "over time these imprinted energies and behaviors become unconscious reactions as applicable to the moment." Tom's thoughts drifted from that moment, to other 'rules' he had learned while a child. Many started with "good boys, big boys, or bad boys" followed with a behavior often permeated with some moral undertone like big boys don't cry. Fortunately for Tom, he had realized that this was pure crap and had nothing to do with being a big boy. He refocused his attention on DocKnow.

"These imprinted energies and behaviors, when incongruent with our true self or with our ability to examine the validity or truthfulness of them, can become stuck in the back of the mind waiting to be resolved. Because these imprints are within us and yet untouchable for our conscious awareness, we tend to project our imprints onto others as a means to try to become conscious enough to bring them into awareness and rectify their incongruence," said DocKnow.

Tom thought about what had been said then asked, "are you saying that much of how we experience other people is actually a reflection of unprocessed imprints within ourselves?"

"Not only that", said DocKnow, "because we all have somewhat similar imprints, we tend to attract others that have some semblance of the same imprints and both at an unconscious level are trying to unravel or dissolve the imprints."

Walks with Woman interjected, "it might be easier to consider these imprints as 'unfinished moments" that have become fossilized or frozen in the unconscious. The importance of these unfinished moments is they continually seek opportunities to become finished. Some call this process compulsive repetition, even though technically there is no awareness of such efforts. If you recall, in earlier discussions, we referred to them as time crystals, moments frozen in a prior time and place that has not been integrated into the overall conscious awareness of the person."

Tom motioned for a time out to give himself a long moment to process what she had said. "So, if I understand both of you, everyone has time crystals. These time crystals are recognizable at some level between people even though it may not be consciously. This recognition is likely through a resonance or some other feeling tone, my words that, in essence, not only attracts such people but seeks to enable both to melt the time crystals and finish the moment satisfactorily. It seems as if we mirror each other" said Tom.

Tom realized he had written something years ago as a poem and had included it in the original Thoughts book that resembled what was being said. He excused himself and went into the house. He walked back and said does this explain some of what we' are talking about. He passed copies across the table to everyone, then read the words himself. Oddly, he decided to read them aloud as he needed to feel the energy or resonance of the words.

### MIRRORS

Sometimes, I look into a mirror and see a thousand faces.

Some are new, not here yesterday nor this day, till now.

Some shimmer with newness while tarnished with despair.

Some glimmer with hope while trying to lighten the ware.

Some are old, buried deep in the furrows of my brows.

Others are cold, frozen amongst the growing scowls.

A few shades the faith sunken in the darkened eyes.

Others are pulled taut from some broken tithes.

Sometimes, I wonder where am I amongst these reflections, then I see one tiny face bursting with emotions spent but not released, and curiously chuckle as thoughts scamper around a childhood lesson of holding on too long and being forced to let Mother Nature run her course.

Sometimes, I look into a face and see a thousand mirrors.

©thstevenson 29 December 89

White Horse seemed to listen intently as DocKnow closed his eyes and Walks with Woman looked into the skies as the words echoed amongst them.

DocKnow smiled. "Seems some part of you has been bubbly up through your poetry writing. Yes, this captures the essence of the reflective quality of everyone's existence. The next piece is to understand that these reflections attract each other to not only thaw the time crystals, moments frozen in time, but to free each person to re-member themselves."

Tom struggled with the attraction and interaction of what seemed an unconscious connection between people that seeks healing. All three watched Tom before White Horse suggested they look into the seven mirrors.

Walks with Woman and DocKnow nodded their agreement. DocKnow suggested, "let's call it a day and start fresh in the morning." No one disagreed especially Tom as he contemplated a new deeper meaning for the poem, he wrote over three decades ago.

# SEVENTEEN: THE REFLECTIONS

Tom awoke early, made coffee and went outside to watch the sunrise. He had learned to sit in the stillness of the morning until he felt a oneness with the sky. Today was one of those days. The contrast between the rising sun and the fading darkness filled his sense of being with a oneness to this moment. A deep sense of gratitude filled every cell within him as his heart opened. He thought, "this is a glorious day."

"Amazing" whispered a voice behind him as DocKnow sat down beside him. "Too bad most people remain in the prison of their minds when they wake up instead of coming out to see the absolute beauty of every sunrise or for that matter every moment." DocKnow added, "you know that sky energetically is a reflection of something inside you."

Tom smiled in agreement without speaking as he was basking in the lingering experience of the moment.

# EIGHTEEN: THE ESSENES

Tom lingered for a bit then realized he needed to get moving. There were animals to tend to, manure to shovel and breakfast to make. He greeted White Horse and Walks with Woman as all three headed for the barn. Over his shoulder Tom noticed DocKnow was sitting with the four dogs each completely attentive to his eyes, his voice, and his touch. It was if all five were in a meditative embrace.

After the chores, DocKnow surprised everyone with blueberry pancakes as well as his favorites of fatback bacon, eggs, hash browns and grits. A fresh pot of coffee was on the table as the only sound was plates and cheeks being filled with delectable mouthwatering food. Tom thought, "we act like we have not eaten in a month, then wondered if DocKnow cooks with complete presence which might explain how wonderful the food tasted."

It took more than a Montana minute to get the group to move let alone clear the tables and do the dishes. Fresh coffee was made as they all sat down in the chairs on the patio. Each took a deep breath and big gulp of coffee while Tom did both at the same time and gagged. He was not pleased with himself. He had spewed coffee everywhere and was coughing like he had taken a deep breath of hay dust.

After settling down, DocKnow said, "we are going to chat about the Spiritual brotherhood called the Essenes."

Tom asked "who?"

DocKnow continued, "many believe that the Essenes were an ancient brotherhood of divinely illuminated beings who believed they were here to share enlightenment with the planet. They were strong advocates of self-mastery and heart-based living. They determined that each moment of our life, the reality of our internal truth (what we have become) is mirrored to us by the actions, the choices, and the language of those around us."

"So, everything is a reflection, just like when you told me this morning the beautiful sunrise was a reflection of something within me" asked Tom.

"That is true," said DocKnow.

Tom asked, "so what do we have these mirrors or reflections."

DocKnow said, "the Essenes believed that we are self-creating all the time, whether consciously aware of it or not. The Essene mirrors are constantly letting us know what we are creating and are endlessly reflecting this back to us."

"For example," offered DocKnow, "when we emit a negative vibration, whether it be a thought, or our voice, the universe shows up for us to support our learning. It gently reminds us of what is going on inside of us and makes us conscious of our creation. When we do not wake up to this and become conscious, the mirror effect increases in its intensity. This would be analogous to failing a test at school and having to re-take a more challenging version of the original, or more applicable to us, learning a life lesson and not integrating it, so that it repeats more vigorously until we resolve the unfinished issues."

Tom pondered DocKnow's words as he realized that he was tense all over his body. Considering all of existence or the universe as we often refer to it, as a living interactive energy that reflects the energies we emit in words, voice, feelings and actions was more than a mouthful. Moreover, the fact that it was trying to awaken his understanding of a self-creating world was more than a stretch. Tom inquired, "so you are saying that every energetic expression that I emit goes out into the universe and echoes it back to me. If I am upset, it will echo anger until I am able to move past those emotions?" Tom paused to uneasily hear the response.

"That is correct," said DocKnow.

Ton continued to struggle with the very consideration that he self-created his world every day. DocKnow reminded Tom of the morning sunrise, "do remember how your heart opened this morning as you suspended all judgment and simply allowed yourself to be with the magnificent sunrise?" Tom nodded, and DocKnow added, "the universe or great spirit or God is a simultaneous reflection and co-creation of every aspect of myself."

Walks with Woman with a soft voice added, "the universe or as you might prefer, the Creator does not discriminate upon what it mirrors to us. It is unconditionally reflecting exactly whatever it is that you are projecting outwards – positive or negative. Unconditional existence does not sympathize, it respects your actions and reactions to your existence until you no longer project lower vibrational energies like hate, anger, lust, or even racism. It is a perfect mirror of ourselves until we wake up to the presence of what is present."

White Horse leaned forward with a piercing empathetic voice, "when you're emitting negativity, it does not enable you by taking it easy on you. Instead, it unconditionally stands by you, and believes in you enough that your will get back up again from the challenges that arise via the mirror effect. The Creator relentlessly mirrors back to us so that we can awaken to our self-created world. The Creator or if you prefer the source of all energy unconditionally shows you what you are projecting outward, for your growth and expansion to occur."

Tom reeled at the thought that he was self-creating or had more choices in his being than he had every considered. He held a tight belief that when he could get present with a quiet mind, he could experience the presence of what is present. It never occurred to him that in being fully present, the presence of what is present is reflected as an awareness of his co-creating partnership with the universe.

DocKnow suggested a break as he wondered if Tom might disconnect from the energies being brought into his awareness. Tom sat in a mindless state more blank than in an understanding or knowing mode. He was checked out for a few moments until he got up and went to the used coffee room.

# NINETEEN: WHAT ARE THE 7 MIRRORS

The group busied themselves for a long lunch while Tom crashed into a deep sleep under a tree. When he awoke, he was comforted with big slobbery dog kisses. Tom did not mind as his canine family were deeply embedded in his day-today existence and to his heart.

When they had finished lunch, DocKnow suggested a walk and talk for the afternoon. This was pleasantly welcomed by all. As they entered the woods, DocKnow looked at Tom and said, "we live in an action-reaction world of our own creation, where consciousness creates reality. We manifest and magnetize people and events into our lives according to our conscious awareness. The Seven Essene mirrors is a way of understanding how this process works."

Tom realized that the morning session was continuing, and he was not sure if he was experiencing a mind stretch, mind bend, or mind fuck. He suspected it was the latter was he felt a bit nauseous as his mind was signaling like the Robot Model- B-9 on the TV series Lost in Space, "danger, danger, Will Smith" whenever an alien encounter occurred. Tom knew that whenever he was leaning into something that threatened the controlling paradigm within his mind, he felt this way. He paused and walked over to lean against the closest tree, a long needle pine. The other's realized that Tom needed a long second to regroup within himself. They all stopped and found a tree to sit under. White Horse noticed that Walks with Woman, DocKnow and himself were under the canopy of a grove of hemlock. He chuckled at the appropriateness and synchronicity.

# TWENTY: REFLECTION OF YOURSELF

DocKnow suggested they stay in this location and asked Tom to come over under the hemlocks when he felt comfortable. Tom scooched himself away from the pine tree, feeling grateful for the calming effect he had experienced leaning against the tree. He slowly crawled over to the others, thinking he was more like an infant while learning the Essene mirrors.

DocKnow proceeded and said, "Mirror #1: What you see outside of you is an exact reflection of what you are in that moment. Your Presence. It is the core of how you see who you are." He paused to see if he was pouring water on a rock or if Tom was absorbing at least some of the energy and information.

Tom took a few deep breaths then said, "the first mirror shows my unfinished business in the moment...err what is reflected to me about me by others in the moment. It seems like it is what I am radiating in the moment based on my life experiences and meaning making capabilities. Any moment frozen in time, unfinished, reveals itself in the other person as a reflection of myself. It is how I have constructed myself to feel safe or whatever dopamine trigger I have created to feel better."

Tom paused as if to take a deep breath and to surrender to the moment as if to allow in the deep knowing he had within himself. He continued, "it can be a reflection of regrets and wounds from my past that I have buried in my unconsciousness, behind the meaning making protective responses, I have created until able to reveal my unfinished business to myself?"

DocKnow smiled and said, "yes, the mirrors are reflecting both your conscious and unconscious mind to create self-awareness of your creative adjustments made to experiences and energies beyond your mind's capacity to process. These often come from childhood experiences that led to creative adjustments to feel safe or prevent feeling like you were dying, like existential annihilation."

The forest seemed to enfold the four of them in total stillness. They sat in silence, like the Still point, allowing the possibility of something emerging to hold them. They sat as One until DocKnow got up and waved for them to walk further into the woods. They walked.

# TWENTY-ONE: JUDGMENT

They walked through the forest for a distance before DocKnow raised his arm to stop and listen. It seemed as if he was listening for something in the stillness. Then, he waved for all of them to sit down. DocKnow remained standing. It seemed he was searching or waiting for something to arrive. Suddenly, out from under the brush appeared a mother skunk with her five little ones following in a row. All sat in the stillness, knowing that the aromatic conditions would change like a fast-moving storm if the skunks were disturbed or scared. Once they passed, DocKnow chuckled to himself while Walks with Woman, White Horse and Tom wondered how he knew the skunks were close. All were glad he did stop them as the alternative would have been a pungent experience.

They walked another fifty yards to the path that goes down into the glacial rocks and cliffs when DocKnow suggested stopping for a rest and conversation. Once everyone got comfortable, he said, "Mirror #2: You attract what you judge or cleverer the universe through others mirrors to us that which we judge in the moment."

Tom quickly responded, "do you mean that we attract people and behaviors that reflect our judgmental-ness?"

"Yes," said DocKnow, "it is the core biases and self-righteous judgements imprinted on us by others or that we develop on our own. For example, if you haven't forgiven people when they make mistakes, you'll see the same behaviors and energies more and more until you realize you should be forgiving. If you really hate it when people talk during movies, you may attract that into your life so that you can deal with why it upsets you. It is something we have been negatively impacted in the past and have not forgiven."

Tom had to mull over the subtleties of this mirror. He understood that if he held a bias against specific behaviors, then he needed to realize that the repetitive occurrence of meeting people with these energies or propensity to behave a specific way was due to the attracting qualities or energies both people were carrying or holding. The stronger the judgementalness, the greater the attraction.

DocKnow continued, "it is good to discern; however, if we judge and condemn with an emotional charge, we will attract exactly what we judge into our lives. You will often see this occur in a pattern format in multiple areas of your life if you pay close attention. A sort of Groundhog Day that is a pattern that occurs over and over. This repetition is the signpost that we have an incomplete experience or tangled energy that seeks integration with the whole of our energy field."

Tom smiled inside as he realized he was beginning to understand this mirror. Then suddenly, he realized he was co-creating these encounters and therefore he was responsible for his emotional reactions to the various people, places and events that led to his outbursts. Tom said, "our judgementalness based on our engrained biases, some passed down for generations, create most of our difficulties."

"Precisely" said DocKnow, White Horse, and Walks with Woman in unison.

Walks with Woman added, "there is a vast difference between judgement and discernment. Most people would say they are discerning when in truth they are judgmental. The process of discernment involves going past the mere perception of something and making nuanced judgments about its properties or qualities and does not include applying assumptions completely different to harbor charged judgements about anything. In the case of a charged judgement, it often comes out in self-righteousness such as blaming them for some imaginary experience or raging upon them for not treating them with regality. Paradoxically, anything that is emotionally charged or that one is internally resisting.......is what you're feeding. It happens simultaneously as a repetitive function that seeks closure to something unfinished inside ourselves. Hence, if you have an internal critic, it is a hint that you are judging the reflection of yourself seen in the mirror of the other. It can manifest as a judgement against the other person or against yourself."

Tom found a brave moment and said, "when I find that many people show me the same pattern of anger or fear... then they may be showing me an internal truth in the moment that I am unable to consciously claim about myself?"

"That is correct," said White Horse. "When we become aware of repetitive patterns by paying attention to recurring energies within ourselves, we can reveal the judgement or unfinished business seeking resolution. The judgementalness in any form begins to dissolve."

DocKnow added, "any time that multiple new relationships appear within the same month, there, likely, is something to learn about how you are about to change or having been resolving old issues. As we dissolve our judgements, we attract the next set of mirrors, often in the form of new people, places, or things."

Tom could not help himself and said, "this feels like a never-ending story of trying to clear the house of mirrors within myself."

DocKnow smirked, "welcome to the path of self-awareness. Self-awareness requires cleaning or clearing the mirrors of our contrived perceptions so that we can truly experience the fullness of the presence of what is present."

Tom was pensive as he was scouring his memories of the times that he had had recurring emotional responses to other people, whether it be their energy, their words, or their beliefs. He felt the reactive responses to each memory then he looked up and said, "we're doing a deep dive into the meaning making aspects of the ladder of inference and the creation of perceptions."

Tom quickly looked up and realized that White Horse, Walks with Woman, and DocKnow were not with him. As he sat there realizing that he was having an epiphanic moment all alone, he heard twigs breaking behind him as all three were running through the woods carrying the making of a picnic lunch. He was glad to see them and the food as he continued to deepen the integration of his profound insight.

They spread a blanket and set the food on a makeshift table of the baskets and sat down to eat. Tom laughed as DocKnow was completely absorbed in a cup of coffee.

# TWENTY-TWO: LOST AND FOUND?

After a hearty lunch of turkey sandwiches, chips and coffee, all four packed the dishes and trash into the basket, they stowed the basket under a tree with a group promise for someone to remember to collect it on the way back to the farmhouse. Tom had an image that they would all forget and laughed to himself.

DocKnow asked White Horse to talk about the third mirror. White Horse looked Tom in the eyes then glanced over to DocKnow and Walks with Woman and then said, "Mirror #3: The third mirror will show you something that you've lost, given away, or had taken away. For example, if you recall, we chatted how we create compromise traps for ourselves and feel like we have given away something that we later regret."

Tom nodded remembering several events in his life where he had mistaken his desire for being a team player while being pressured to take short cuts on a work project, which he still regretted. The memory felt like a "no win" paradox of being damned if he did and damned if he didn't. He sensed this mirror was going to reflect some clarity that he had not been able to see.

"This third mirror is an Essene mystery of relationship that is reflecting when we sense we find ourselves in the presence of a person who, when we look in their eyes, you feel an electrical +/- charge." Said White Horse. "When we see something that we love and desire in another, it is often something we have lost, given away or had stolen in our own lives. Every relationship is a relationship with self and often we try to reclaim what was lost, we gave away, or had taken away as a child. It could be joy, innocence, honesty and integrity, courage, or love. All of which can be reclaimed within self. On the dark side, this mirror can be seen when we feel jealous or envy."

"Time out" exclaimed Tom. "So, you are saying everything is a mirror of our internal world of self-created perception including all relationships. This self-created set of perceptions also has an unconscious aspect of when we have missed the mark with who we are, resulting in a desire or strong inclination to resolve this lingering unfinished business. Through the course of our lives, we give away or lose parts of ourselves. When we find ourselves in the presence of another individual who embodies what we have lost, we will feel it as a +/- magnetic connection to that person. It can feel positive or negative."

White Horse nodded agreement.

"So, when I feel these energies whether attracting or repelling it is a good time to pause and ask myself, what is it I see in this person that I have lost, or I've given away or was taken from me?" said Tom.

White Horse continued, "if you've lost, given away or had something taken from you, you may keep seeing others who have that thing or situation. This may result in an attraction (spark) towards someone that you don't know why you're attracted to them. The attraction is because they have something that you want in your life, such as a good job, or family, etc. These situations will come up to make you deal with your regret that you don't have it. You are unaware consciously of this regret, which is why your subconscious is bringing it to your attention. Once you are conscious of it, you can make a choice to go after the thing you want or choose that you don't want it enough to change your life. Once you make a conscious decision one way or the other, the spark should go away."

DocKnow added, "We will seek to restore that which we have lost, given away or had taken away, consciously or unconsciously if it is congruent with our true self."

Tom remembered that over the course of the last three decades, he had intuitively understood this mirror. For many months during meditation, he set an intention for all lost, forgotten, stolen, broken and misplaced parts of himself to return to his awareness so that he could integrate each and restore wholeness to himself. Over the course of months of daily meditation, insights had begun to surface and had enabled him to find a sense of wholeness within himself. Admittedly by accident on his part or a conspiracy of his subconscious and the creating universe, these intentions had healed several fragmented times of his life.

The four of them decided to return to the farmhouse as it was getting later in the day and chores needed to be done. As they walked through the woods, Tom noted how soft footed all four were walking. There were no sounds of breaking twigs or rustling leaves. In fact, there was no indication that anybody was walking through the woods.

Like a fading dream, he remembered that often when he would take men into the woods for alone time, he would walk the deer paths and quietly check on each man just before darkness. Typically, his appearance scared the bejesus out of them as he seemed to suddenly appear beside them. Just as quick the memory was gone.

# TWENTY-THREE: LOST LOVES

Somehow, fried chicken, mashed potatoes, green beans, corn, and biscuits were on the table after chores. White Horse hinted that somebody did a Kentucky Fried Chicken run and quickly redirected himself to the delicious smells on the table. When all had finished, DocKnow checked on everyone over dinner. Everyone noted they felt energized after eating so DocKnow proceeded for one more Mirror.

Mirror #4: A Forgotten Love

DocKnow freshened his coffee, then said, "The Fourth Essene mystery or mirror of relationship reflects (back) to us our most forgotten love. This could be a way of life, a lost or unfinished relationship. Often it is a past life where a wrong conclusion from past experience was created. These will recreate themselves over and over until the right conclusion is registered in the soul as wisdom."

Tom choked at hearing the correlation to past lives and lost loves. When he calmed down, DocKnow continued, "through the course of our lives often we will adopt patterns of behavior that become so important to us that we will rearrange the rest of our lives to accommodate this pattern or behavior. When we find ourselves in this situation, we find that these patterns may be codependent, compulsive or addictive patterns of behavior."

Tom interrupted DocKnow. In a voice that seemed to echo through time, Tom said "my first marriage was a bewildering

journey of missing each other. My wife struggled with an addiction to pain killers which led to some severe codependent behavior on my part. I did not
understand the excessive use of the drugs was an addiction and this explained the wide-ranging emotions of the relationship."

"One night" he continued, "I had a lucid dream where I was a mortally wounded native American. My wife had tended to me as I died. Having never seen a fair skinned woman, I has assumed that she was some sort of spiritual being that I felt grateful and indebted. When I woke from the dream, I realized that at some time or in some ancestral imprint, I was carrying an indebtedness that did not need to carry over through different lifetimes. I had proceeded to support her addressing the addiction. She was not interested. I shared the dream with her, and we both knew the marriage was over."

DocKnow waited for Tom to leave the memory and come back to the table, then he continued, "as you clarified Tom, the fourth mystery allows us to see ourselves in the presence of codependence, addiction, or compulsion. Through codependency, addiction, and compulsion, we give away little by little the things that are most important to us. And in the giving away, we have the opportunity to see ourselves as we lose the things, we hold most dear; typically, ourselves."

Tom inquired, "so codependency, addiction, and compulsive behaviors try to fill a void from something lost or never gotten in this life, such as the need for love or to be seen and heard at a soul level in search of existential validation."

DocKnow nodded and continued "the pattern gradually unfolds over time. We give away what is most important to us over time… our self. We may recognize the pattern and heal, at any time, and find our wholeness in the healing. It requires conscious awareness in the present moment."

Tom recalled that during the marriage he had had a sense of

being empty that slowly dissipated after the divorce. This lesson reminded him to trust what is true within himself instead of compromising in ways that trapped him. The love he had lost was that of himself.

# TWENTY-FOUR: PARENTAL IMPRINTS

The next day, Tom walked into the kitchen to the smell of fresh coffee and an assortment of pastries. Of course, DocKnow was sitting at the table eating a Bear Claw, a humongous one. He seemed completely absorbed by the presence of what is present in his mouth. Tom smiled, he'd only seen such culinary pleasure by a few people, often when eating chocolate.

DocKnow, while licking his fingers, suggested they sit outside on the patio when they started this morning. Tom did not see Walks with Woman or White Horse, so he assumed they were out doing errands and something else. He grabbed a large coffee and a smaller bear claw Danish and sat out in the morning sun. As happens, the four dogs came running and Tom was able to get about a ¼ of the Danish as they got the rest. When he said, "all gone" and showed both sides of his hands, whatever attentiveness they had had for him was gone. They turned and ran off to the other side of the house to chase squirrels.

Tom was semi-meditating or napping depending on your perspective when White Horse and Walks with Woman pulled up in the truck. They had been at the grocery store, and apparently had gotten a lot of food. DocKnow nodded to them as they walked into the house to unpack the supplies. Tom wondered why they had gone to the store when there was a lot of food in the house.

Everyone got their coffee. Walks with Woman and White found the Danish and brought theirs to the patio with big smiles.

DocKnow followed with another large Bear Claw. When he saw Tom look at him, DocKnow smiled, shrugged his shoulders and in one mass movement, plopped into a chair, while taking a bite of the bear claw. It was not an act of grace as he spilled half of his coffee. Everyone smirked except DocKnow who simply ignored everyone and kept eating his bear claw.

When everyone seemed satisfied and coffee mugs were refilled, Walks with Woman initiated the conversation, "the Fifth Essene Mirror is perhaps the single most powerful pattern. It is the mirror that our parents showed to us through the course of our childhood and lives with them. It is through this relationship with our parents that we are shown ourselves in that expectation and beliefs from those relationships. For example, if we find ourselves in a relationship with our parents where we feel judged, constantly. Or that we feel that our best is never good enough. There is a high probability that what is being mirrored is our belief within ourselves that we may not be good enough. Or that we may not have accomplished what may have been expected of us. It is an external imprint that can be released through our perceptions of ourselves and our creators, our parents. It's a powerful and subtle mirror. And it may tell us more about why we've lived our lives as we have than any other image."

Tom understood this mirror in more ways than he preferred to acknowledge. In very positive ways, he had learned many of life's requirements from his parents. His family were hardworking folks. Pop had worked three jobs to make ends meet. There was no complaining, just the commitment to feed and clothe the family. Everyone was required to do chores and learn how to take care of themselves, learning to do laundry, cook, and the nightly dishes.

At ten, Tom was required to do odd jobs to make enough money to buy his annual school clothes. He recalled that he was not exactly on board with the idea of working, especially assuming responsibility to get the work done on someone's else schedule. Later, he realized that this requirement had become one of his better lessons in life. There was no animosity about responsibility or working, though he did struggle with raging bosses. At about 40, he decided to be independent and start his own business. He had had a moment of remembering that Pop had told him once, "find something you really enjoy, you will be doing it a long time." With that in mind, Tom had decided that he would only accept work with people or organizations that were fun, interesting, and challenging.

Tom returned from his memory as he looked up to see three faces looking directly at him. Tom smiled, and said, "I had a moment."

Walks with Woman continued, "there is a good possibility that the words (positive and negative) you have used to describe your parents have very little to do with those you call Mom and Dad. With those words, you are describing a mirror. This is the mirror your parents have held to you of the most sacred relationship you will experience. The way you see your Mother and Father (the words you use) of this world is a mirror of your expectations (supporting or disappointing) of the relationship."

Tom stuttered a moment or two, then said, "over the years, I have realized that I was repeating the exact words of my parents or behaving the same ways as they did in similar situations. I realized that these were energetic imprints that were modeled and expressed in my presence, and over time, I began to examine them for truth or resonance within myself. Some things I have kept and others I have let go."

Walks with Woman nodded to Tom then added, "the appearance of our father or mother, reflects our relationship with creation. It is often said we marry our father or mother. We also often become them acting out the same healthy and unhealthy patterns we learned as a child. This is to work through the unfinished and incongruent energies that reside in our unconscious. Our fathers and mothers to us as children are Gods. So, we accept without question what was modeled and expressed towards us."

Tom seemed to stair into the eyes of Walks with Woman before saying, "even though I had acknowledged that my parents physically created me, I am seeing it is much more than that. I had accepted many aspects of who they were through mimicking their behavior and creating energetic resonance with different practices." As if doing a life review, Tom continued, "I realize now that I resonate strongly with my father concerning healing energies and practices. In being in the presence of what is present when he healed burns, those energies resonate within me as I have adopted or accepted them as part of myself."

He continued, "I am sensing that I am in the process of a spiritual reckoning within myself. Over the years, I referred to my mother as religious as she found solace in the sanctuary of the church and my father had found it in nature. As a young man, I had gone to church as expected by my mother as she worried about my soul." Tom smiled, I found no relevance to the people and the teaching as at a very young age I struggled with hypocrisy. I felt averse to religion and held strong emotions against it. I was not sure if Jesus existed at least in the ways professed. In the last few years, I was introduced to Neil Douglas Klotz, Prayers from the Cosmos who has translated the original Aramaic texts to English for such texts as the Lord's Prayer. Using his translations, I wrote my personal version of it." Tom shared his version with them.

| | |
|---|---|
| Our Father which art in heaven<br>Hallowed be they name<br>Thy kingdom come<br>Thy Will be done in earth, as it is in heaven<br>Give us this day our daily bread<br>And forgive us our debts, as we forgive our debtors<br>And lead us not into temptation, but deliver us from evil<br>For Thine is the kingdom, and the power, and the glory, forever.<br><br>Amen | Eternal source of all being<br>Hallowed is your emanating presence<br>That fills me with clear intention for cocreating life.<br>Unite me with your eternal presence<br>Nurture me with self-awareness<br>By showing my misdeeds and misunderstandings<br>And revealing the clear path of Oneness<br>Through being a healing presence to myself<br>And all that I encounter.<br><br>So be it! So, it is! So, I am! |

After a few minutes, Tom continued, "when I initially read the translations, I had a profound energetic release in my body and especially my heart, with a deep knowing that my long standing perceptions and relationship with the energy of Jesus Christ had completely changed. I realized it was not the spiritual concept of Jesus but the energetic resonance with the numinous Christ energies that mattered." Tom looked around the table and said humbly, "I have not been the same since that experience. I have somewhat understood that the Creator energy is within everyone regardless of religion."

Quietly almost reverently DocKnow, White Horse, and Walks with Woman stood up and walked into the house. Tom sat quietly realizing that he had not expressed that experience and realization to anyone. He also realized it not only recreated that original feeling it also made it feel more real now that he had shared.

# TWENTY-FIVE: LOOKING INTO THE VOID

After the break, Tom noticed that Walks with Woman and White Horse were packing food and camping gear into the utility vehicle. DocKnow noticed Tom's curiosity and said, "we are going to spend the rest of the day and tonight in the woods."

At first stunned, Tom shook his head as if he was not able to make the transition of going to the woods, then he spurts out, "of course," as if what else is going to come into awareness.

As soon as they packed, White Horse and DocKnow took the utility vehicle into the woods. Tom and Walks With Woman agreed to meander through the woods until they found the other two. At first, it was walking in the stillness, which Tom had difficulty determining if the stillness was in him or the woods. The morning conversation had brought more into his awareness the journey he had been on the last few years. He accepted that his 40-year journey to find himself had revealed many insights into how he was being impacted by all that he came into contact with. Moreover, he remembered a time that he had fallen into a deep darkness, a void, that lasted a year. During that time, he had drafted many poems as a journey deep inside himself. He recalled two that seemed to describe the beginning and the slow recovery from that place full of fear and eventually to the discovery that he was a self-creating being.

# Loss of Self

I used to write letters of encouragement, notes of happiness,
and thoughts I wanted or maybe needed to share.
I used to sense when someone's heart needed a lift knowing
that it would lift my own when I reached out to them.
I used to know when to be silly, sad, and occasionally
mad without knowing or caring why.
I used to hear the songs of the soul whispering in the swaying trees,
the rustling leaves, the buzzing bees, and deep within me.
I used to smell the roses blooming below the window,
the noodles dancing in the kettle, and the life celebrating
within each breath as a glorious gift to myself.
I used to taste the life within each sip, each bite, each savoring chew
until they were replaced with gulps, belches, and meals on the run.
I used to touch the earth in reverence grateful for the
nourishment, warmth, and care it gave to me.
I used to see what was not seen within each set of eyes, string
of words, and roll of emotions as reality and not illusion.
I used to believe that I was filled to the brim as a pool of joy, anger,
love, and sadness until I realized that the pool was empty.

©thstevenson
24 August 94

He recalled being in a dark space, like a void, where he was getting clear about himself and his life, much of which he realized was more fabricated than coming from the center of himself. As he recognized that he more than the contrived sense of himself, he had discovered that he was much more than he had every considered as a person.

### Dread

With an archaic regard, I stand before you curious and with great awe.

All around and deep within feels like the touch of darkness at the bottom of a naked well, where life has dragged me to this place of utter despair, where waves of desperation roll over and over and over, where the coldness makes even my soul shiver.

"I have been here before" filters through my mind less comforting than a memory and more matter of fact than a thought.

"I wonder" crosses my lips more like a plea than a curiosity and floats away like a leaf dancing in the air as it falls from the tree on its only journey, returning to the earth.

Twirl, float, twirl, twirl, float, twirl, float, float, the words know where they are going and yet dance with total disregard like a ballerina lost in the flow of life.

"I wonder" begins to simmer like a black hole of the soul wherein nothing matters but this moment, this moment where all that has been vanishes into dense darkness.

"Get Real" startles even the gods as the thunderous voice of the naked darkness reminds me that I am not a guest nor even an innocent bystander.

Terrified, fear explodes from my pores like cold sweat burning from a fever until I drop into the eternal depths and forthrightly bow surrendering to the starkness, yielding to what is, knowing that in this single act I acknowledge that which has always been and take my place within the darkness, my darkness.

©Herb Stevenson, 2007

He realized that the darkness within himself must be embraced if healing is to be accomplished.

# TWENTY-SIX: CAPABILITY TO FACE DEEPEST FEARS

Walks with Woman reminded Tom to pay attention to this world and not the internal one while walking through the woods, "those trees will only sway so much before they let you run into them to wake you up," she said. Tom abruptly looked up and saw DocKnow and White Horse carrying the gear down into the lower level of the farm where the glacial rocks and cliffs were located. Tom wondered why they were building camp down there instead of up top under the hemlock grove. "Oh well," he mumbled knowing that he was in for an adventure.

All four worked together to build a makeshift camp. Instead of tents, tarps were strung together to create a large lean-to shelter with the fire on the outer edge. Smoke would rise out the front while some heat would move to the tarp and radiate to the back of the shelter. Basically, it was designed to keep the chill between reasonably cold and reasonably warm depending on what was happening within the person.

The finished setting up camp wile White horse was cooking up a pot of white bean chili with chicken and more than a large touch of red pepper and jalapeños. Tom chuckled to himself as he knew there was no milk, or cream to ease the burn if White Horse got too carried away with his recipe for internal burn to keep warm at night.

The chili was tasty and DocKnow had revealed a fresh corn bread to round out the dinner. All seemed good.

After cleaning the dishes and burying the scraps to minimize animal intrusions during the night, they sat around the fire. They decided to tell a few funny stories. Tom noted that one year, he had brought a group of men to the woods for a weekend retreat. Part of the experience was to find a place for alone time. Tom had walked around checking on each person and noted one guy had set up on a ledge overlooking the cliffs and glacial rocks where they were sitting. Walks With Woman, White Horse, and DocKnow all looked up at the same time and in unison said, "hope he bounced" as they anticipated that he had fallen overt the edge. Tom laughed and said, "he did not fall; however, he had built his space over a snake nest. As I was telling him he should move back from the ledge so as to not fall over once it got dark, a 5 foot black snake crawled out of its nest where he was sitting on the ground. Suddenly, he took off crawling on all fours faster than I could run to catch him. He was making so much noise, everyone in the woods heard it and had a restless night worrying about snakes."

All four were laughing until their eyes were watering and their bellies hurt. White Horse asked, "why didn't you tell him that it's not harmful?"
Still wailing with laughter, Tom said, "I couldn't. I was laughing so hard I could barely run."

They continued to tell stories for about an hour, then DocKnow said "we should get started" as he added a log to the fire.

White Horse said "okay," then said, "the sixth mirror is a reflection of our journey and search into the dark side, the denied aspects of ourselves. Some say it reflects (back) to us the Quest for Darkness or what is often referred to as the Dark Night of the Soul."

Tom realized that his recall during the walk into the woods of the dark period in his life was not coincidental, maybe synchronistic and likely triggered by some part of him that sensed the next mirror. He sat quietly listening to White Horse.

"The Sixth Essene mystery or mirror of relationship is when we meet our greatest challenges, our greatest fears and have been gathering the tools and understandings in life to confront them. These reflections are the repressed parts of us that have been condemned or vanquished and are reflected-back to you by people or circumstances that show up in your life. As you heal each memory (a single memory) you heal the universal fears."

1. Fear of not being good enough (worthy).
2. Fear of trusting (internal authority) and surrendering (allowing in).
3. Fear of abandonment (belonging) and separation (existential aloneness)"

Tom shared the poems from years earlier in his life and how they had been terrifying at first and later became the most insightful time of his life.

DocKnow asked, "what was your initial experience?"

Tom said, "one night I went to bed and had a lucid moment that if I died in the night, I would be content because at 38 years of age I had accomplished more than I ever thought possible. I fell immediately into a deep sleep. The next morning it felt like I had not awoken to who I was the night before. My work required detailed recollections for which I was suddenly aware that I knew answers to client issues and frightfully I had no access to the information. I felt like I was witnessing a part of me fading way into oblivion." Tom could feel the terror rising in his body as he recalled the year long experience.

DocKnow suggested that Tom look in the eyes of everyone sitting here to refocus himself. Tom did so with many deep breaths, then continued. He recited the poem Dread and explained that the turning point was when he realized that his own fear and terror was the darkness of himself being reflected back. When he accepted that the fears were of his own creation, insights into how he had created his life completely incongruent with his true interests, beliefs, and desires He began to examine and eventually reconstruct himself.

Tom looked at DocKnow and said, "now I understand your diagram of the evolving and emerging selves. I needed to evolve for the true self to emerge." Everyone nodded.

After a break to water the tress, White Horse continued "if we have a negative person or experience that we are very energized in their presence, we want to work out what this is mirroring to us and how it is representing a deep or disowned element of ourselves in some way. As you just explained, Tom, once we can own this darkness buried deep in ourselves, there is room for deep healing to take place."

DocKnow added, "on a side note, the deepest, most rejected parts of yourself are often what you can be unconsciously most attracted to in a partner! The purpose of this is for you to see yourself in your entirety, so that you can integrate and be whole."

He continued, "we are reminded that life has a propensity toward balance, nature has propensity toward balance. It takes an extremely skillful and masterful being to upset the habitual balance in our lives. When we find ourselves in the greatest challenges of life, it in those moments that we may be assured that the only way those challenges are possible is after we have amassed each tool that will allow us to move through that challenge with grace and with ease... until those tools are amassed, we will never see ourselves in the situations that ask us to demonstrate these high levels of mastery."

From this perspective, the greatest challenges of life, may be viewed as tremendous opportunities to demonstrate mastery of ourselves as a living presence, rather than tests that may be passed or failed in life. It is through this mirror that we see ourselves naked, without the emotion and feeling and thought and constructs around us that we have assembled around us to keep us safe. We can see ourselves in a naked way and prove to ourselves that the process of life may be trusted."

Walks with Woman in a solemn voice added, "This mirror is an opportunity to lose everything we've held dear in life and see ourselves naked in bare witness of ourselves. As we climb out of the abyss that is left after the loss of everything we held dear, we see ourselves in a new way; this is where we find our highest levels of presence."

The four of them decided to call it a night. All got into their sleeping bags and listened to the stirring animals in the woods. Tree toads had filled the air at dusk and now the sound of critters walking the woods and Owls hooting echoes deep into the distance of Tom's mind as he floated into sleep.

# TWENTY-SEVEN: FINDING OUR TRUE SELF

Tom woke up to the sound of drums. As he sat up, he realized that he was dreaming. Sitting around the fire in their luminous bodies were DocKnow, White Horse, and Walks with Woman. Tom was startled. "Is this some kind of movie from Rocky's Horror shows," he thought?

All three smiled and said, "glad to see you could join us. We wondered if you were ever going to fully awake?"

Tom looked around as the drumming softened and he noticed many others sitting on the glacial rocks and cliffs smiling and welcoming him. He sensed these were those that had come become and created ceremony in this space thousands of years ago,

He felt that drums resonating deep within him as if massaging his heart. Suddenly, he had vivid memories of doing a drumming circle 30-40 years ago. One night, after the drumming, a gentlemen said, "I am a heart specialist, oddly with a serious heart condition. I started coming to these circles more out of a deep sense of needing to be here and not knowing why. For three sessions, I have not said anything. Tonight, I wish to speak. Every time the drums played, I would go into a deep trance like experience, where the drums massaged my heart. The first night, it removed the stresses and tensions from doing myself instead of being myself. The second session released all of my regrets, compromises, and heartaches. Tonight, I have clarity about who I am. I am healed and will not be back." The medical doctor proceeded to get up and walk out the door.

Tom was confused. He was not sure what was going on. In a flash, he was sitting up in the darkness with the other three all snoring and not in the drum circle. Unsettled, he could not go back to sleep as he struggled with what had just happened. An old familiar fear of getting lost on the other side or what modern medicine called psychosis exploded from his pores.

Just as quick, he remembered having struggled through the massive psyche explosive energy releases that seemed to blow apart his sense of reality. Totally, unsure of what was real or that he could even trust what was real, he had contacted his spiritual big sister, Fran, a therapist and told her the feelings. She referred him to another friend, a psychiatrist. After meeting with Fred, he was prescribed an antipsychotic drug. In somewhat of a daze, he went to a pharmacy and got it filled. Tom recalled the pharmacist looking at the prescription and giving a very odd look at Tom. In a spontaneous moment, Tom realized that his fear of going or being crazy was over. He understood that filling the prescription created a record that he was certifiably crazy. As he walked out of the pharmacy the moment turned into hilarity. When he got home, he placed the prescription bottle on the monitor of his computer and used it to remind himself to not take everything so seriously. He realized that without all his culturally imposed fears, he was more sane than ever, well, mostly. He suddenly recalled, that in the days that followed, he had drafted a poem.

## The Space Between

I have many faces.
Faces for work,
faces for play,
faces for whatever

I think that I
might need one.
Do not be confused,
for these are not masks.
Masks are surreal,
whereas my faces are not.
They are me
in all
of my facets,
until one day I no
longer need it.
Then, it becomes a mask
that served me well.

©Thstevenson
April 29, 2002

Tom focused on being fully present in this moment, in the woods, under a tarp shelter with three close friends. In time, he allowed himself to relax into the night until the others awoke. He was confused and yet excited. He was not quite sure what all had happened during the night. He simply knew it was an opening to something beyond himself or not.

# TWENTY-EIGHT: SELF-PERCEPTION

To Tom's surprise, White Horse was shaking him and saying, "come home little Sheba." Tom was surprised and disoriented, he thought he had stayed awake after all the events of the night before.

DocKnow offered him some still camp coffee and warned, "this will make you see things in the night" as all three laughed. Tom was not humored and was pleased to get the coffee. Besides hot; he thought, this will make you bark at the moon.

After they finished an amazing camp breakfast of bacon, eggs, pan baked biscuits, they packed the kitchen and settled around the fire.

DocKnow paused, then asked, "Sleep well?"

White Horse and Walks with Woman were intently watching to see what Tom would say.

"Well, I feel like I went on a WTF trip of some sort." Said Tom. All smiled in a wise knowing way which more disconcerting than supporting. Tom felt like his experience was affirmed and that did not sit well inside him.

He shared what he had experienced Walkes with Woman, White Horse and DocKnow listened intently as he recalled his night. DocKnow asked, "how are you making meaning of it, all or part.?"

Tom said, "overall, I wondered if I was in Alice in Wonderland going down a rabbit hole, maybe of self-discovery. At other times, I felt so discombobulated that I was not sure if I could find my own ass with either hand."

When the three digested what Tom had said, they burst into laughter as the visual was both appreciated and absolutely belly tickling.

Walks with Woman brought the group back to a calm place and said, "the last mirror or mystery is about self-perception. It seems your experience were awakening and reminding you at the same time. Understanding what happened to the doctor was a reminder of having witnessed someone reframe their sense of self-perception in liminal space. Your memory of the pharmacy experience reminded you that your self-conceived perceptions had filled you with unfounded fears that were dissolved in a moment of presence. Sitting in your luminous body with all of us seeks to understand that we are more than our physical bodies. To think it true is one thing, however, to experience it as true is another completely mind-bending experience that requires keeping your wits about yourself to the presence of what is present."

Tom recognized what was being said was true while he had an echoing sense of knowing. He said, "many years ago, I was with Rosalyn Bruyere where she did two mind bending events. The first involved Walks with Woman. Walks with Woman smiled, and said, "yes, my eyes were slightly wider than normal, and she used energy to shift the patterns of my facial structure and move both eyes in to the more normal spacing."

Tom said, "As I watched Rosalyn and Walks with Woman, the eyes moved closer to the center. At the time I thought it was an optical illusion."

"As you can see" smiled Walks with Woman, "it was not. The shift has been permanent."

Tom said, "later that day Rosalyn created a massive energy field. She had noted that such high frequencies are difficult to be in and if your capacity to expand you vibration is not large enough, you will fall asleep. I had thought about hocus pocus until she started. She was channeling an Abbott from the Bon Po from some era many millenniums ago. As I watched, I began to see her shapeshift in the luminous body of an Asian man. He was larger than Rosalyn, so her body expanded, and her hand size doubled. My mind was going bonkers and unable to make sense of it. So, I asked Walks with Woman what she thought about the hands expanding. To my surprise, she said, "amazing how big they got" which was not the answer I had wanted. She affirmed and my mind struggled to determine what was real."

"Later, I chatted with Rosalyn and told her how vivid the image of the man, and she said, 'because the image is energy that you recognize, you likely knew him well.', whereupon I had a second gaps for what is real." said Tom.

White Horse asked, "how do you make meaning now?"

"Recalling those events now," said Tom, "I realize that my sense of what is real far exceeds most people. And, I am realizing that for the most part every one has a limited sense of what is real or not including within themselves and with what we call reality. I am gathering that last night was a way to frame break my perceptions of what is real including within myself. At this moment, I am comfortable with everything that happened as if something has dissolved or no longer exists within myself."

DocKnow, jumped up and said bio-break, and ran off into the woods. Others went into different directions as mother nature calls cannot be ignored.

# TWENTY-NINE: APPEARANCE OF SELF-PERCEPTION.

When they returned to the camp, DocKnow started the conversation after passing out bear claws that he had stashed in his pack. "The last mirror is the mirror of your self-concept both conscious and subconscious. It defines what is real within and without."

"The most difficult aspect to grasp and embody is that the seventh mirror reflects (back) to us our self-perceptions. Others will perceive and treat us according to how we perceive ourselves. People will show up in our life to mirror to us how you treat yourself. This might be the most powerful one, because we aren't always aware of how we are showing up in the relationship to ourselves. For example, if you constantly hear yourself talking about how people 'take advantage of you,' chances are you're taking advantage of your own time, resources or energy to please other people. The people that show up in your life and 'take advantage' are your teachers, mirroring to you exactly how you treat yourself, or believe about yourself."

"Similarly, if we have low self-esteem and do not acknowledge our wisdom and beauty, others will not acknowledge them. If we are angry, bitter, and unloving to others, they in turn will often react in the same way towards us. If we change our perception of ourselves, we change the world. Maybe it is time to be kind, loving and compassionate to ourselves and others."

"As you learned last night, what we believe to be true or real is also self-created perceptions that can be expanded, bent, or dissolved. Bent perceptions are ones we are unable to shift so we feel internalized bruising. Expanded perceptions are epiphanies that expand our self-awareness. Dissolved perceptions are a liminal experience that irrefutably shift the sense of what is real without any need for external approval. It feels like an immutable truth" said DocKnow

# THIRTY: RE-MEMBER

The energy of the moment shifted and without any cue, the four of them began taking down the tarp shelter and packing the gear. Everything was stowed in the utility vehicle and Walks with Woman and White Horse were headed out the woods and back to the farmhouse.

DocKnow sat down with Tom and said, as you process what you experienced, discerning what happened is better than judging what happened. Judgment adds an implicit moral dynamic of right/wrong, real/unreal that is like repeatedly driving down a dead-end road 90 mph only to remember that there is a brick wall just ahead. Stay with your experience in descriptive terms not prescriptive judgements.

Remember:

1. Every mirroring event is an opportunity to recognize yourself more clearly. Pain or frustration guide us to the fragmented part of ourselves that are calling for integration.

2. When on autopilot, you are not consciously creating. Whatever programs you picked up on in childhood are instead creating on your behalf. The more intentionality we can bring to each moment, decision, emotion and thought, the more we flow with the current of life.

3. The more aware we are in each moment, the easier it becomes to recognize the lessons that the universe is bringing to us.

4. The mirrors become more and more subtle as time

goes on.

5. Allow for perfection in the imperfections of life.

6. Focus on the presence of what is present by asking what I am not willing to see in this moment."

Tom and DocKnow stood up and walked quietly to the farmhouse.